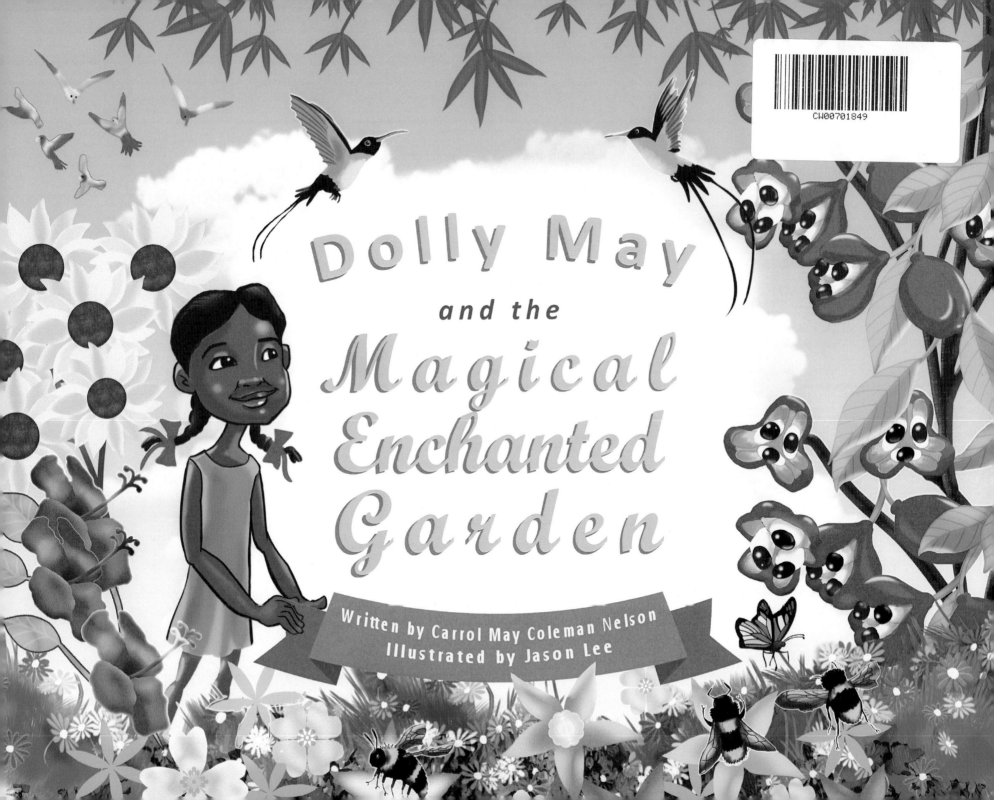

Dolly May
and the
Magical
Enchanted
Garden

Written by Carrol May Coleman Nelson
Illustrated by Jason Lee

Children's Fiction

Copyright © 2019: Carrol May Coleman Nelson

First Printed in United Kingdom 2019

Published by Conscious Dreams Publishing
www.consciousdreamspublishing.com

Cover Design by Jason Lee
www.jasonmation.co.uk

Typeset by Oksana Kosovan

Edited by Daniella Blechner

ISBN: 978-1-912551-52-1

DEDICATION

To my wonderful parents Catherine Adina Coleman

and Glenford Adolphus Coleman

who are forever in my heart.

Contents

CHAPTER 1

The Magic of Mount Olive

Mount Olive is situated in a misty, mystical mountain range of Ginger Ridge in Jamaica. Mount Olive is surrounded by undulating hills and a magnificent flamboyant bamboo backdrop and every day a gentle morning breeze wafts by. If you look carefully, you can see Mount Olive glowing in the morning sun.

The mountain has always been covered in luscious leafy vegetation, fruit trees and verdant pastures. It is home to goats, cows, donkeys and horses who graze on the plentiful morning dew.

Surrounding it, is a gentle flowing river, shimmering streams and plenty of fish to feed the kids. Legend has it mermaids lived there too. It was a playful place for fathers and their sons to fish, while little girls like to play happily catching tadpoles and throwing stones.

But the best part of Mount Olive was that it was also home to Grandma Majji's magnificent and beautiful garden that was full of magic and mystery to Dolly and her friends. You could always hear the twittering and humming wings of the magical doctor birds and stripy bees among the flowers and the trees, working hard in the rising sun.

Grandma Majji looked after the land and its verdant pastures with bounteous and plentiful crops rich in ackee and avocado, rose and star apples, bananas and breadfruit, cashews and coconuts, mangoes and naseberries. Majji's magical garden was just like her. It held a sense of magical beauty and wonder which spanned around the house and local villagers loved to come and visit. Sometimes Majji allowed Dolly to lend a hand, picking fruits and vegetables. Majji made her world and their world one.

CHAPTER 2

Grandma Majji and her Mystical Garden

The entrance to the house from the narrow country lane led to Grandma Majji's magical garden. In the garden, was an awesome ackee tree with its alluringly colourful display of fruits of yellow flesh. Inside each yellow fruit, was a bold, black and dazzling shiny seed that took the centre stage.

The house was surrounded by magnificent red and orange rose brushes, perfect poppies, lustrous lilies and sweet-smelling shrubs. The most extraordinary of them all in the summer was her symphony of stunningly beautiful, golden, skyscraper sunflowers. The daring beauty of her sunflowers dazzled the passers-by.

'Sunflowers are magical,' said Majji.

'Why?' asked Dolly.

'Dear child, they resemble the life-giving sun. They come to bring us lasting happiness,' replied Majji.

Majji had a slender frame with long, wavy, silvery hair and a smile that captivated Dolly. Dolly was a happy, inquisitive and bright little girl with eyes that sparkled like a star. She loved spending time with her grandmother in the garden.

Grandma Majji gently took Dolly's hand and they wandered through the garden.

Heavenly hibiscus and pretty primroses lured the beauteous doctor birds, ladybirds, bees, butterflies and the enchanting fireflies that added to its never-ending magic.

But Majji's favourite was the Tree of Life.

'This plant, my beloved Dolly, holds the magic to life here on Earth,' Majji explained.

Majji attended to it every day picking little pieces for us to chew on as we wandered around the garden.

CHAPTER 3

Majji and the Maattinees

The little deities who lived at the top of the mountain, Joycee, Leetee and John, Donna and Dolly, Jen and Pearl, Junior and Peggy loved to meet up and play with the new children, Matthew, Sophia and Jay, Mally and Jay-Jay from the other side of the mountain. They wished the day would never end. They called Grandma *the Majji* and she called them *the Maattinees*.

On Mount Olive, the sky and the fields were aglow as the Maattinees played in Majji's garden filling the surrounding mountain with wonder.

Majji always seemed to have an understanding of what the Maattinees liked. Some of the Maattinees liked to run up the hills to be the first to reach the garden, some skipped merrily on their way with excitement.

Magnificent Majji always had a basket full of coconut candies, coconut drops, sweet potato pudding, jackfruit or roasted breadfruit, rose apples, star apples for the Maattinees. The Maattinees loved Majji's authentic kindness.

Majji's garden was full of life not just from her beautiful flowers and trees, birds and bees but the bustling activities of the Maattinees. They enjoyed jumping around and playing games like 'tag' with each other sometimes breaking a flower stem or two of one her beautiful roses, hibiscus or sweet pea or disturbing Lizzy the lizard.

The Maattinee boys like to whistle and the Maattinee girls like to giggle. Some of the boys pulled out wiggly worms to frighten the girls, whilst some girls liked to look for ladybirds. Some liked to search amongst the flowers for four leaf clovers and caterpillars. One liked to play at the end of the garden with her pretend friend Benny. Another liked to play hide-and-seek under the pretty poinsettia tree. Another just liked to scribble and draw on his slate whilst nudging Majji 'Look! Look! Look what I have done for you!' he'd exclaim excitedly. Majji would always reply in her soft magical voice, 'Oh that is beautiful, you my dear child is a great artist.'

The Maattinees loved her beautiful words of praise which poured from her mouth.

CHAPTER 4

Dream Big

Majji loved to play a game with the Maattinees called *Guess Who I Would Like to Be?*

'Who would you like to be?' Majji asked the Maattinees softly as they gathered to play in the garden.

'I would like to be a doctor,' said John and Junior as they rushed around the garden with the wiggly worms, chasing the screaming girls.

'Ah!' said Majji, 'You can be a great doctor like Dr Martin Luther King Jr. who was one of our greatest world Civil Rights Leaders for justice and peace.'

The Maattinees stared in wonder.

'He made a famous speech called *I have a dream* in which he described a vision of one day living in a world where people are no longer judged by the colour of their skin, but by the content of their character.'

'I want to be a leader!' Matthew said gleefully.

Majji was amazed by their imagination. 'You can become a world leader like President Nelson Mandela who was a world famous South African human rights activist, political leader who fought against apartheid, Nobel Peace Prize winner and President of South Africa,' Majji said, her eyes opening widely.

'Guess who I would like to be Majji? A Scientist,' said Donna and Pearl as they danced around Majji.

'Me too,' said Leetee.

As Majji was passing around the fruit from her basket to the children she embraced the girls, 'My dear children you are so remarkable and can be a great scientist like Katherine Johnson, Mary Jackson and Dorothy Vaughan.'

'Who are they?' asked the Maattinees in their surprised little voices.

'These women were NASA's black mathematicians who worked for the Apollo Space Programme. They helped to send John Glenn, The United States' first astronaut, to space. He flew the Friendship 7 Space Mission to orbit the earth.'

CHAPTER 5

Beyond the Stars

As the afternoon went on, the Maattinees continued to play their favourite game with Majji.

'Guess who I would like to be?' exclaimed Sophia who ran swiftly unto Majji's arms.

'I would like to go above the sky to see the stars.'

'Ah well my dear child, you can be like Dr. Mae Jemison NASA's former astronaut who was the science mission specialist on the STS-47 Spacelab-J. This eight day mission was accomplished in 127 orbits of the earth, a cooperative mission between United States and Japan.'

Jen and Peggy jumped up with their jolly voices. 'We would like to fly a plane!'

Majji looked over with her knowing look and reassuring voice. 'Well you two can be like Bessie Coleman, a pioneering female in the field of American Civil Aviation. She was known as the world's greatest female stunt flyer and parachutist.'

Junior exclaimed, 'I would just like to see the bottom of the sea!'

Majji expressed joyfully to Junior that he could be a deep-sea diver and study the Coral Reef of our beautiful island, as she marvelled at his vivid imagination.

Jay shouted to out Majji from behind the ponsietta tree where he was enjoying his adventurous hide and seek game with Mally and Jay-Jay. 'When I grow up, I know just who I want to be.'

'Now tell me, who you would like to be!' said Majji as she peered over towards the tree.

'A writer!' said Jay very boldly.

'Me too! Me too! Me too!' said, Mally and Jay-Jay as they ran over to Majji.

'You would make great writers,' said Majji, 'like Derek Walcott, a Caribbean Nobel Prize winner in Literature whose writing span poetry, theatre, journalism, painting and teaching.'

'Another is Dr. Maya Angelou who was awarded numerous prestigious awards. She was presented with an Honorary Doctorates by more than 50 universities and colleges for her work as a civil right activist, poet, actress, movie director, producer of plays and teacher.'

CHAPTER 6

Have Courage

t was nearly time for the Maattinees to go home. Just before they went on their way, Joycee and Dolly leapt up from their game of hop scotch and said 'We want to be nurses!'

'How wonderful!' said Majji. 'Of course children. You can be a nurse like Mary Seacole who left Jamaica and went to nurse the soldiers in the Crimean War. Her application to join Florence Nightingale's team was refused so she funded the trip herself. This incredibly brave women rode on horseback in the battlefield, even when under fire to nurse wounded men on both sides of the war. One of a kind nurse.'

In Majji's magical garden, their imagination filled with wonder.

Majji often shared her wisdom with them all. On this occasion, Majji quoted a special verse from Dr Maya Angelou, *'The most important virtue is courage.'*

It was finally time for them all to go home, Majji said, 'Maattinees, when you grow up you must have courage and we can be like anyone of these great people and more.'

They looked at each other in wonder.

'We are to study and learn well at school so the gates of knowledge and wisdom shall be open unto us, as there are no limitations to what we can achieve,' she continued.

'We will have our dreams realised and become phenomenal men and women and help our beautiful world.'

THE END

ACKNOWLEDGEMENTS

To my wonderful mum and dad who are no longer with us.

My wonderful grandma and her magical garden, which gave me the opportunity to experience great beauty and magic in nature.

My wonderful aunt Merlyn aged 93, who was a school teacher and introduced me to a love of books and writing at a young age which helped shape me to be the person I am.

My three wonderful children Matthew, Sophia and Jay who are my source of inspiration and keep me grounded and supported me in creating this book.

To my wonderful aunt Dell, my sisters, brothers, cousins Joyce, John, Donna, Pearl, Denise and niece Andrea for love, support and positive words of encouragement.

My circle of strong friends, family and the sponsors who through their generous contributions helped me to bring my dream into a reality. Also to authors Mumba Kafula and Merline Ulysse who introduced me to Daniella Blechner and enabled me developed my writing.

To Daniella, who gave me the opportunity to attend her *Power of Your Story Workshop*, which led to the creation of this book.

Thank you to My Book Journey Mentor, Daniella Blechner's Conscious Dreams Publishing Team.

Thank you to Illustrator Jason Lee for bringing the book to life through his amazing illustrations and patience.

Thank you to Claire Lockey for her amazing press release and PR assistance

Thank you to Oksana Kosovan for typesetting my book beautifully.

To my supporters Jenessa Qua, Frances Beaty, Dorothy Forde and daughter Vanessa, Hyacinth Nelson, Sadie McClue, Sophia Nelson, Jay Nelson, Tom Nelson, Matthew Nelson, Patricia McCollin, Veta Squire, Barbara Duncan John, Angela Brown, Hazel Wallace, Lyn Gilpin, Claudette Coleman, Elaine Coleman, Dorcas Bridge, Verna McLean, Andrea Nelson, Dianne Nisbitt, Paulette Bailey, Tana Thomas, Lola Nelson, Surriya Walters.

Thank you all.

About the Author

Carrol May Coleman Nelson lives in Manchester but spent her early childhood growing up in the beautiful countryside of Mount Olive, Ginger Ridge, on the Caribbean Island of Jamaica.

As a child, she resided with her grandmother whilst her parents move to the UK in search of economic freedom. Later, she lived with her aunt Merlyn, her husband and their children due to her grandmother's ill health and later joined her parents. She grew up with a love of books and writing introduced to her by her aunt Merlyn who was a school teacher and encouraged by her younger sister Claudette.

Carrol's background is Public Health Nursing, Cognitive Behavioural Therapy, Mentoring and Coaching. Whilst studying her BSc in Nursing and working with disadvantaged children and young people in the care system, her passion for writing was reignited. Carrol's wish is for children and young people to feel empowered to pursue their dreams and transform their lives.

Lightning Source UK Ltd.
Milton Keynes UK
UKRC022227270619
345149UK00001B/3